S0-BSZ-660

ALISON WALKS THE WIRE
by Sheri Cooper Sinykin

Illustrations by
Gabriel Picart

Spot Illustrations by
Rich Grote and Catherine Huerta

MAGIC ATTIC PRESS

Published by Magic Attic Press.

Copyright ©1996 by MAGIC ATTIC PRESS

All rights reserved. No part of this book
may be used or reproduced in any manner whatsoever
without written permission except in the case of a
brief quotation embodied in critical articles and reviews.

For more information contact:
Book Editor, Magic Attic Press, 866 Spring Street,
P.O. Box 9722, Portland, ME 04104-5022

First Edition
Printed in the United States of America
1 2 3 4 5 6 7 8 9 10

Magic Attic Club is a registered trademark.

Betsy Gould, Publisher
Marva Martin, Art Director
Robin Haywood, Managing Editor

Edited by Judit Bodnar
Designed by Susi Oberhelman

ISBN 1-57513-066-1

Magic Attic Club books are printed on acid-free, recycled paper.

As members of the
MAGIC ATTIC CLUB,
we promise to
be best friends,
share all of our adventures in the attic,
use our imaginations,
have lots of fun together,
and remember—the real magic is in us.

Alison   Keisha

Heather   Megan

Contents

Chapter
One

ALISON'S
SECRET

Alison McCann was just shoving the last pile of sports magazines under her white wicker bed when someone banged on her door. "Come in, Mark," she said without looking. Her mother's knock was as soft as an apology, her father's was more like a private code, and the twins always came barging in, so it had to be her older brother.

"Mom wants to know if your room's all cleaned up and whether you're done with your book yet. I'm supposed to tell you—"

"I know, I know." Alison didn't even want to think about how many pages she still had to read before school started the next day. "Tell her my room's so clean now, I can't even find my book!" She scrambled up from the floor and looked at her brother purposefully, hoping he'd take the hint and leave, but all he did was smirk.

"I bet I can find it," Mark said, reaching for her closet door. Alison lunged and made a grab for his arm. But she was too late. The louvered door swung wide, unleashing an avalanche of sneakers, rumpled clothes, papers, and sports gear. "There," Mark said, crossing his arms smugly, "does that help?"

Alison pursed her lips and glared at him. "Do you know how long it took me to get all that stuff put away? Do you?"

Mark raised one eyebrow. "Wouldn't take any time at all if you just got yourself organized."

"Yeah, well, not everyone is as perfect as you."

"Ah, so you finally admit it."

Alison plucked a couple of old sweat socks off the floor and pelted Mark with them. It would serve him right if hers smelled worse than his usually did, she thought. "Go on, get out of here!" she yelled. She tried to shove him out into the hall, but he wouldn't budge.

Instead, he turned on a phony screech that sounded

exactly like one of the twins. "Mommy, Mommy, help! Ali's hurting me!"

Alison made a clucking sound with her tongue and turned away, disgusted. She didn't have time for this. And she wasn't kidding about the stupid book being lost, either. Her best friends Megan Ryder, Heather Hardin, and Keisha Vance, had each probably finished the two-hundred-page summer reading assignment weeks before—make that months before in Megan's case. Alison knew that there was no way she could join them for one last vacation adventure in their neighbor's attic until she'd finished reading hers, too.

"Ali," her mother called from somewhere down the hall, "leave Stevie and Jason alone, do you hear me?"

Alison's mother couldn't even tell that it was Mark trying to get her in trouble. Indignant, Alison eyed the mess on her floor. *Just get yourself organized.* Easy for Mark to say. That was part of her problem and he knew it. Alison supposed her parents meant well by explaining everything to her brothers. But just thinking about the reading specialist's findings—and the humiliating little family talk that had followed—made her cheeks burn all over again. For the past six weeks she'd tried so hard to put it out of her mind.

"Hey." Mark tapped her arm. "What I said before—I'm sorry. I forgot all about your—"

"Don't say it."

"What? Learning disability? Jeez, Ali, it's no big deal."

"Yeah? Well, you're not the one who's . . . " Alison's voice trailed off. She still couldn't bring herself to even say the words aloud. She, Alison McCann was *not* learning disabled. It really bugged her how the rest of her family was so quick to believe that she was. She was class president, captain of her soccer team, the first person picked whenever sides were being chosen, and she did pretty well in school.

"Come on." Mark surveyed the mound of Alison's belongings, then knelt down and began sorting them into small piles. "It's not as bad as it looks."

"No, it's worse," Alison replied, and despite her best efforts not to, finally cracked a thin smile of gratitude. While she didn't want her brother's pity, she could use all the help she could get. Two pairs of hands—and eyes— were much better than one. Maybe together they'd even find her book.

With exaggerated patience, Mark talked Alison step-by-step through the cleanup. She was beginning to think she liked it better when he was teasing her. At least that made her feel normal, like the old Alison whose report cards said "is making progress in reading" instead of "has fallen below grade level."

Finally, Alison wadded the last unwanted piece of paper and shot it across the room into the wastebasket next to her desk. She glanced at her alarm clock. Considering that she read at a turtle's pace and that her book was still lost, she'd never have enough time, no matter when she was supposed to meet her friends. She knew she shouldn't have put off her assignment for so long. Even if Mark found her simplified version of *Little Women* that very minute, even if Jason didn't make Duke bark, even if Steven taped his mouth shut and tiptoed through the house until bedtime, to Alison reading sixty-three pages in less than a day seemed impossible. It would be easier to swim the English Channel.

Chapter
Two

UP A TREE

Mark soon found Alison's book mixed in with the magazines underneath her bed. It was hard to stay angry with him after that. "Thanks for trashing my room," she teased.

Mark grinned. "Anytime. That's what big brothers are for." He hesitated in the doorway. "Oh, yeah, I almost forgot. I was also supposed to tell you that Mrs. Haggerty called. She has to change to Mondays, whatever that means."

"Starting when? Tomorrow?"

But Mark had gone. With a great sigh, Alison closed her door and lay down on her bed to read. But her thoughts kept wandering back to Mrs. Haggerty, the private tutor her parents insisted she work with once school started. That meant tomorrow. Monday. They sure weren't wasting any time. What was she going to tell her friends when she couldn't walk home with them after school? She'd have to think of something, because the truth was just too embarrassing.

"Read, Ali! Concentrate!" she scolded herself. She began the sentence again, this time out loud. "'Jo was Laurie coming up the walk.' No way! It must say, 'Jo saw Laurie.'" She plowed on. But soon every little noise seemed amplified. The stupid tick of her clock, a basketball hitting the backboard over the garage, the twins thundering down the hall—all throbbed in Alison's head like her own heartbeat. "Aaaargh!"

Grabbing her book, Alison stormed from her room to the den, but Matilda's loud purring proved as distracting as a power lawn mower. The kitchen and nearby family room were out of the question, too. Her mother was clattering pots and pans and dishes as she emptied the cabinets so she could put down new shelf paper. Groaning with frustration, Alison gazed beyond the French doors to the backyard. She'd give anything to be out there right now, doing something, anything.

At the sight of the tree house, Alison punched the air in victory. "Mom," she called over her shoulder, "I'll be up in the fort, okay? Don't tell anyone, except Heather, Megan, or Keish."

Alison wasn't sure how long she'd been reading. Long enough to outgrow the tree fort, it felt like. Her back ached and her stomach was growling, despite the egg salad sandwich her mother had brought her earlier. She paused to riffle the remaining pages. Good. At least she was getting somewhere. Anyway, it wasn't as if she didn't already know the story's ending. She and the rest of the Magic Attic Club had watched the video together at least twice at Megan's sleep-overs. If only Alison had seen it before their first trip to Ellie Goodwin's attic, though, she wouldn't have felt so out of it when Megan suggested they "play *Little Women*."

Who would have guessed that with one look in Ellie's mirror, she and her friends would be traveling through time on the first of many incredible adventures. And who could have imagined that they'd form something as cool as the Magic Attic Club on their return?

"If you want to go up to the attic today, Alison McCann," she reminded herself in her mother's sternest voice, "then you'd better stop daydreaming and finish this book!" Forcing her eyes back to the page, she had to reread the whole paragraph to remember where she'd left off. Why did looking at a bunch of letters have to be such exhausting work, especially when really tiring sports felt more like play? Alison thought about the specialist's comment that many people with reading problems have trouble with things like dribbling and catching a ball. That made her luckier than most kids, she supposed. Though lucky was definitely not how she was feeling at that moment.

"Hey, Ali! You up there?" Keisha called.

Alison set her book down, looked out the tree house window, and replied with a shrill whistle. Her friends hurried across the freshly mowed lawn.

"Think we can all fit?" Megan asked, squinting up at the sturdy tree fort.

Alison suspected that she, Megan, and Keisha still could. But they hadn't played up there in a long time, and Heather never had. "I don't know. But we could give it a try."

"That's okay," said Heather. "I'll stay down here."

"No way!" Keisha laughed. "You just want to have us all up a tree so you can run next door and get first dibs on an outfit."

"You really think I'd do that?" Heather's grin reassured Alison that she hadn't taken the tease the wrong way.

"The truth is," Heather admitted, "I'm not much good at tree climbing."

"Then it's about time you learned. Right, Keish?" Megan came up beside Heather, and she and Keisha gave Heather a boost.

"Don't let me fall!" squealed Heather, her arms in a death grip around the trunk, as Megan and Keisha pushed from behind.

Alison leaned down, grasped Heather's wrists, and hauled her the rest of the way up.

"Thanks, guys," Heather said once Megan and Keisha had managed to squeeze inside the fort. "Am I the only one who's scared of heights?"

"You call this high?" Alison tried not to scoff. When it came to reading, she reminded herself, Heather could just as easily make fun of her. "We're packed in here like sardines."

Sitting sneaker to sneaker, knee to knee, each back against a wall, the other girls nodded. One by one they caught the giggles, making the whole fort tremble.

"Whose bright idea was this, anyway?" asked Keisha finally. "I thought we were going to Ellie's attic."

"You all go on," Alison said, trying to sound unconcerned. "I still have to finish my reading for tomorrow."

"You're kidding, right?" Megan pretended to pout. "Ali, we've been planning to go to Ellie's all week."

"I know. I'm sorry." Alison shrugged helplessly. "It's just that with soccer starting up and my brothers always around—she broke off, wanting to tell them the whole truth, but it wouldn't come—"well, anyway, what's done is done, and what's not is not. Guess you may as well go on without me."

"I wish there was something we could do to help," Keisha said.

"Me, too," replied Alison glumly, "but there isn't."

"What're you reading, anyway?" Heather reached for the book in the corner, but Alison, embarrassed that she wasn't reading the "real" novel, caught her hand.

"It's nothing special. Look, why don't you guys just go? The sooner I finish, the sooner I can join you."

Heather looked from Megan to Keisha. "Well, see you later." She watched the two girls scramble backward out of the fort, then hesitated as if she wanted to say something more.

Alison wanted to as well, but Heather turned away to face the others and the height that had so unnerved her.

"Jump!" Keisha called. "It's not as high as it looks."

To Alison's amazement, Heather jumped. Inside the treehouse, an unspoken challenge seemed to hang in the air. Alison nodded, accepting it. Then she picked up her book and began to read.

C h a p t e r
Three

MONTY'S CHOICE

After dinner, Alison holed up in her room, determined to finish *Little Women*. The day had seemed like the longest in her life. But a promise was a promise, and she couldn't break one to her new teacher or to her parents.

Every time she checked her clock, the big hand was pointing straight up. But at last, exhausted yet strangely energized, too, she slammed the book closed. "Done!" She immediately raced to the window. It was still light

out, but only barely. Just time enough to go to Ellie's—
the perfect reward!—and be home before sundown.

As Alison approached the white Victorian house, all
the windows were dark. She frowned and hurried up the
front steps. When no one answered the bell, she opened
the screen door to knock. A sealed envelope with her
name on it fell at her feet.

Alison ripped it open
and struggled to make
out the handwriting: *The
girls said you might come, but I
need to visit a sick friend. Would you please let Monty out and check
his water? You know where the keys are. Love, Ellie*

Alison grinned. For once she'd have Ellie's cute little
terrier all to herself. Maybe she'd even take Monty with
her through the mirror! She knew Ellie wouldn't mind.
Taking the house key from its secret hiding place, she let
herself in, turned some lights on, and called for the dog.
His nails clicked across the hardwood floor. "Come,
Monty, come!" Alison made two quick kissing sounds.
"And *up*!"

Monty bounded forward and leaped into her waiting
arms. "You're such a smart boy," she said as she touched
her nose to his rough, wet, black one. "You want to come
to the attic with me?"

Monty licked her cheek, and Alison giggled. "Well, okay, then. But first we do what Ellie said." The terrier cocked his head as if he understood, and Alison let him out the back door. When he returned, she took the golden key from its silver box and climbed the stairs to the second floor two at a time, Monty close behind. After unlocking the door to the attic, she made her way up the final steps.

Hot, moist air pressed close about her, making it hard to breathe. But once she had tugged on the familiar satin pullcord of the hanging lamp, bathing the attic in rosy light, nothing seemed to matter but the old steamer trunk filled to the brim with unique and colorful outfits.

"What's it going to be today, Monty?" asked Alison. "Something totally outrageous, okay? I'm up for a great adventure, aren't you?"

Monty woofed and went straight to the nearby mahogany wardrobe, where one door stood ajar. Alison tapped her foot impatiently, certain he'd find nothing good in there.

"Over here, Monty!" She clapped her hands, then plucked at several shimmering outfits in pinks, purples, and white. Even if dogs couldn't see colors, surely the movement would catch his eye. "Look here, boy! Look!"

Monty ignored her. When he came to her at last, he was dragging something red and shiny, all edged in gold—a cape, maybe. Dropping it at her feet, he went back to get something else. It looked like a crown.

For effect, Alison tried them both on and finally announced dramatically, "Queen Alison of the Attic! Ta-da!" Monty was sitting at her feet like a loyal subject. But she was surprised to see a little pile of outfits there, too. As she examined them, Monty whimpered. "Looks like this is for you, isn't it, boy?"

Alison fastened a ruffle around his neck. That left a red leotard, short skirt, gold wristbands, and soft red slippers for her. She quickly changed into them, then shook her head. "I haven't a clue what I'm dressed for, Monty," she said. "I'm trusting you big time. This better be good."

She picked the dog up and stood in front of the tall, gilded mirror."Wow! Look at us, Monty! Are we a team or what!" She turned to admire the cape, and as it billowed out behind her, a strange low, churning noise filled her ears. Monty trembled and buried his head under her arm.

Alison wrinkled up her face, wishing she could hide

from the motorlike roar, too. But now the distinct odor of fuel oil assaulted her. It was mixed with the musty smell of hay. The combination seemed unnatural—even dangerous. Goose bumps erupted on her arms. Turning back to the safety of Ellie's attic, Alison realized all at once that it was gone.

Chapter Four

DIZZY IN THE BACKYARD

A lison's reflection bounced back at her from several mirrors on the side of a lavishly gilded red circus wagon. The words *Corbellini Circus* were carved prominently across the top. She walked around the wagon, trying to get her bearings. It was always so confusing to just drop into another time or place.

A counter protruded beneath an open window, marked by a sign that said TICKETS. Besides the constant low humming, which she now saw was made by a huge, smelly generator, Alison thought she heard voices. They were coming from a big-top tent that seemed to have been raised in the middle of nowhere.

"Oh, Monty! This really is a circus! Good job, boy!" She held him as she made her way through the arched canvas entrance tunnel. It led to stands of bleachers and a ring covered with blue tumbling mats. There, a man and three young boys were rehearsing some kind of balancing act, using a small trampoline. Alison ventured closer, hoping Monty wouldn't do anything to startle them.

"Daddy," one little boy said, "is that the girl Aunt Dizzy's looking for?"

The man motioned for the children to wait in the ring, then approached Alison with his right hand extended. "Stefano Corbellini," he said, "and you are . . . ?"

"Alison McCann, and this is Monty." Alison waved the terrier's paw, then suddenly realized her own mistake. She was supposed to shake Mr. Corbellini's hand. Way to go, Ali, she thought. He's probably the boss. "Sorry, sir. It's just so exciting to be here." Her hand felt tiny and soft in his rough, callused one.

"You studying with my sister, Belinda?"

"Um, uh . . . ." What exactly did he mean by studying?

"Belinda Serrano. Or maybe you know her as Dizzy?
Are you her new wire walker?"

A wire walker! Fantastic, Alison thought. "Oh, yes, Mr.
Corbellini! That's who I am all right. And Monty here, he's
going to be part of my act."

"Well, we'll see. The real Mr. Corbellini—my father—
will have the last word on that."

Alison nodded. How many Corbellinis were there,
anyway?

"You call me Santo, okay? Like you're part of the
family. And your name again is Alison?" Santo shook his
head as if he disagreed, then smiled. "That won't last
long. You go with Renzo now, okay? He'll help you find
Dizzy in the backyard." He pointed to a
boy about Alison's age.

How could a circus have a
backyard? That and other silly
questions tumbled through Alison's
mind. She didn't want to make a fool
of herself by asking even one of them.

Thanking Santo, she hurried after
the boy. He parted the tent flaps on
the far side, revealing a campground or

a parking lot, Alison wasn't quite sure which. The support wires from the tent seemed to form a huge spider web. Fluorescent orange tape marked the spots where they were staked in the ground so that no one would trip.

"Watch out," Renzo warned her. "Don't clothesline yourself." He scratched Monty's ears, then pointed out two rows of trailers and RV's. "Aunt Dizzy's is the big silver one at the end. On the left, okay? Just look for the lady with the real clown hair. You can't miss her."

Alison nodded as if she understood, then thanked Renzo, set Monty down, and started off. Heat waves shimmered off the metal motor homes, turning the sky a split-pea yellow. A sudden, fierce thirst quickened Alison's pace. She hoped Dizzy wouldn't think her rude, introducing herself and asking for water in the very same breath. A baby cried in one trailer; a boom box rapped from another. Somewhere bratwurst sausages were grilling, sending up the best smell of summer in a white trail of smoke. When she stopped at the trailer Renzo had described, Alison swiped her forehead with one wristband, then knocked on the door.

"I'll get it, Dizzy," a young woman's voice sang out.

Alison's knees twitched despite her best efforts to stand still. When the door opened at last, Monty charged up the front steps and past the muscular, dark-haired young woman who smiled down at Alison. "Hi. I'm Gina, Dizzy's niece. You're Alison, right?"

Alison nodded, then apologized for Monty.

"It's okay. He's probably thirsty, and I'll bet you are, too. Come on in. Have some lemonade or something."

Alison stepped up into the trailer, surprised that the place was air-conditioned. To her right was a sofa and love seat, where Monty had already made himself at home among the bright quilted pillows.

"Atta girl," someone said, "keep pushing those fluids. Can't tell you how important it is when the weather's like this."

Alison turned. Closing a pocket door to what appeared to be a bedroom was a middle-aged woman with hair so curly and unnaturally red that Alison realized at once what Renzo had meant by "real clown hair." Dizzy's eyes were lined with dark pencil and her cheeks were heavily rouged. But there was nothing phony about her smile or the way she found Alison's hand and squeezed it.

"I'm so glad you're finally here." Dizzy took a seat on the sofa, and patting the cushion beside her, invited Alison to sit, too. "Time's getting short, and as I told you, I'm in great need of an apprentice."

Gina returned with a glass of lemonade for Alison

and a plastic tub of water for Monty. Alison chugged the tart drink gratefully.

"Doesn't her costume look great, Diz?" Gina asked.

"Sure does. But I think you'd better practice in just your leo," she told Alison. "Save the glitz for when you've earned it."

Alison stood and hurriedly stripped off everything but the red leotard. "Okay," she said, "I'm ready."

Monty jumped off the sofa and nudged Alison with his head. Me, too, he seemed to say.

"Not quite, boy." Alison laughed as she removed his ruffle. "There! Now can we start? Where's the tightrope? How high is it? Can Monty be in my act?"

"Whoa, Speedo. Not so fast." Dizzy winked at Gina, then turned again to her new apprentice. "First you've got to pass a test."

"A—what did you say?" Maybe Alison had misheard. All the same, her stomach knotted with apprehension. Wire walking sounded like fun. Why wouldn't they let her get going?

Chapter
Five

STEP-BY-STEP

ou mean the binocular test, Diz?" When her aunt nodded, Gina, grinning mischievously, disappeared into the back of the trailer home.

Alison gave a quick sigh of relief. She knew all about using binonculars. They came in handy at football games. Sometimes, after a huddle broke, she could almost read the quarterback's lips.

Moments later, Gina returned with Alison's "test." "I remember when you made *me* do this, Diz," she said.

"What was I, ten? eleven?"

"Then you were my age!" Alison exclaimed, glad to discover that she and Gina had something in common.

"Yep. Half my life ago. And I still can't decide whether I want to go to grad school or finally join the circus."

Dizzy cleared her throat. "Maybe Alison here'll be a natural, Babycakes, and you won't have to make a decision at all."

Alison looked from Dizzy to Gina, trying to figure out what each one was hoping. Then suddenly Gina was all business, motioning Alison to get up from the sofa. "First of all, it's called a wire, not a tightrope," she said, handing her the binoculars.

"Wrong end, Speedo," Dizzy whispered when Alison put them up to her eyes.

"Nuh-uh," Alison said. She wasn't that stupid. "I always look—"

"She means *use* the wrong end," Gina explained gently.

Alison nodded, turned the binoculars around, and brought the wider lenses up to her eyes.

"Now look down," Dizzy said.

Alison obeyed. Incredibly, her feet seemed miles away! Was that how the tallest basketball players felt? Like swaying skyscrapers? "Wow! That's so cool!"

"Now take a few steps," Gina said. "Try to walk a straight line."

Immediately, the carpet seemed to spin and move beneath her feet. Alison struggled to keep her balance, and somehow managed to stay calm and not fall.

"See, Gina?" Dizzy's voice held just a trace of smugness. "She's a natural. What'd I tell you? Not a hint of vertigo."

"She's steady all right. Not like me. I practically fell off my feet, remember?" Gina laughed. "So, where to now? The practice wire?"

"Is it okay if I put these down?" Alison asked, still

37

holding the binoculars and marveling at the strange sensation. "Did I pass the test?"

Dizzy laughed and clapped a hand on her back. "With flying colors, Speedo. Time to try the real McCoy."

Monty stayed behind in the cool trailer while Dizzy and Gina took Alison to a practice wire in the backyard. Nearby, a lone elephant chained at the ankle, trumpted their arrival to several circus performers who were lounging in the shade. "Step right up, missy," one said.

Alison stared at the practice wire. Suspended between two trees, it was only inches off the ground. Dizzy launched into a detailed explanation of how a small jack pulley kept the steel cable taut, but Alison, insulted, could hardly listen. Even Keisha's balance beam was way higher than that practice wire, she thought. What did they think she was, a baby? She'd bet that even the poor elephant could walk it if they'd let him! "Isn't it mean to chain him up like that?" she asked. "All he can do is walk in circles."

"He's a she. And let me tell you something." Dizzy squared Alison's shoulders and looked her right in the eye. "People don't understand that that's Magda's security. She knows nobody's going to bother her there."

"But her ankle—"

"We wouldn't dare mistreat her. All her trainer has to do is call, and she'll pull that stake right up and carry it on over to him."

"Really?" Alison's eyes grew wide. What a joke on the public!

Dizzy tweaked Alison's chin gently. "Now, enough about the elephant. Are you ready to walk the wire?"

"That one? It's going to be way too easy for me," Alison said matter-of-factly.

"Some things look easy," Gina cut in, "but take it from me, they're only mastered step-by-step."

Alison wondered whether wire walking would be much different from her favorite sports. Maybe she'd turn out to be a natural, as Dizzy said. "Okay. Tell me what to do."

And Gina and Dizzy did. "Balance on one foot, facing the tree." "Try again." "Ignore your arms." "Don't walk." "Change feet." "Find the balance." "Try again."

Alison tried not to show her frustration. Gina was right—this was a lot harder than it looked. Now that she was up there, the wire felt much higher than a measly few

inches. "How long do I have to learn this?" Alison asked.

"You mean, if you want to be in the show? Two days, right, Diz?" Gina's dark ponytail swung as she turned to her aunt.

Dizzy bobbed her head emphatically. Her red curls bounced like springs. "Yep, just two days left till we try to save the circus. And let me tell you, we'd all better pull star turns for those bigwigs, or—"

"What do you mean, pull star turns?" interrupted Alison.

"Do our acts perfectly," Dizzy explained. "We've really got to impress these business people, or we can forget about winning their grant money—and our plans to stop touring."

"Corbellini's a small touring circus," Gina added. "Mostly family. It's hard competing with the big-name ones anymore."

"But if you stop touring . . . you mean, the circus might fold?" Alison, concerned, stepped down from the wire, but Dizzy waved her up again and told her to fix her eyes on the end and try a crossing.

The cable trembled as Alison stepped forward. How could she concentrate on wire walking when the entire circus could be at risk? Her shaking knees set the wire vibrating in waves that kept getting worse, threatening to pitch her off. Her arms flailing wildly, Alison jumped down. "I just can't keep my mind on this," she said. "Not until you tell me what you mean by 'save the circus'."

Dizzy told her about Circus Corbellini's founder, her great-grandfather Gian-Paolo, and about the family's struggle to keep the circus from folding. But touring was tiring and expensive. And it was harder and harder to "make their nut," an expression which, Dizzy explained, came right out of circus history. It used to mean taking in enough to pay the bills and buy back the

special wagon nut they'd need in order to roll safely out of town. Now it pretty much meant breaking even. Last year the Corbellinis had been forced to let the tiger act go because of the cost of all the meat required to feed the big cats. Magda the elephant would probably be next. And then there were the younger generations of Corbellinis who were choosing to go to college and leave the circus behind for other careers. At this, Gina blushed and hung her head.

"It's all right, Babycakes," Dizzy consoled. "Nobody's

blaming you. We've just got to adjust to the way the wind's blowing, that's all. What we want to do now is go into the schools and teach circus skills in all the gym classes—give every kid a chance to feel successful," she explained. "After each term, the kids would join us in putting on a big show."

"That'd be so cool!" Alison said.

Dizzy nodded. "But everything hinges on getting our first big grant."

"Now I see why this show's so important." Alison's hope of performing in it faded as she went back to the wire. Unless she found her balance soon, there was no way she'd be good enough to help save the circus. With stubborn determination, she fixed her gaze firmly on her goal. Then, she inched forward step-by-step.

Chapter Six

UNDER
THE BIG TOP

B y late afternoon, Alison had graduated to the low wire under the big top. Dizzy shooed the clowns and other relatives out of the tent so "her girls," as she now called Gina and Alison, could practice undistracted. Then she demonstrated how to use a balancing pole, hopped down, and let Alison try.

From the ground, the seven-foot-high wire seemed like no big sweat. But it felt more like seventy once Alison stepped onto it. She had to admit that holding the long, heavy pole firmly in front made a world of difference in her balance.

Dizzy was trying to explain something about the center of gravity and angles, displacement, and force, but Alison couldn't concentrate on a word she said. She was too busy worrying about how she might help save the circus. It would take a miracle—or magic—to even *appear* in tomorrow's show. That she might actually impress the audience seemed more unlikely still.

Gina, meanwhile, was fastened into a harness and safety-wire contraption that Dizzy called a mechanic. With Santo keeping watch as her spotter, she climbed to the highest wire to practice.

Now that's where I want to be, Alison thought. Up there with Monty. She wasn't quite sure what about that wire excited her more, the challenge or the danger. Either way, she realized, at the rate she was progressing, she'd never be ready in time. With a sigh, she turned back to her own wire and focused again on her goal.

Dizzy walked alongside Alison almost within arm's reach, giving equal doses of advice and encouragement. Every once in a while, she seemed to wince. But whenever Alison caught her, she quickly smiled.

"Are you all right, Dizzy?"

"Just fine. And you? Head erect now. Atta girl."

Under the big top, the air hung thick and lifeless. The temperature climbed. Before long, sweat ran between Alison's eyebrows and down her nose.

"Okay, Speedo, that's enough for now." Dizzy directed. "You go on back to the trailer and rest. Take a little nap. I need to work with Gina and practice my act."

"Oh, please, can't I stay and watch?"

Dizzy shook her head firmly. "It's too hot. Bet it's a hundred and twenty up top. You gotta take it slow and—"

"I know, I know. Push the fluids." Alison grinned. "I promise. I'll try. But I've got to warn you, Mom says I flunked naptime in preschool."

How long did Dizzy expect her to rest? Alison turned from her stomach to her back to her side, trying to get comfortable on Dizzy's double bed. Even the bumps on the chenille bedspread bugged her. She was wasting time, lying there doing nothing. So far, Ellie's mirror hadn't given her any special ability. Somehow, Alison decided, she had to make magic of her own.

Her gaze traveled to a blue perfume bottle on Dizzy's dresser, then to the bookshelves beyond.

They were mostly filled with collections of little spoons and porcelain thimbles, with a few books at one end. Curious, Alison pulled the thinnest book out. It was a picture book about a girl wire walker in long-ago Paris.

Alison reached for a thicker book. It turned out to be the autobiography of a famous high-wire walker, *The Great Moreno*. Not many pictures, unfortunately, just sketches, Alison thought. And the print was so small. Judging from the chapter titles, though, all of The Great Moreno's tricks and secrets were fully described. The thin picture book definitely looked a lot easier, but for some reason Alison put it back on the shelf.

"Come here, Monty." She patted the bed, then lay on her side, letting the best light meet *The Great Moreno's* open pages. The terrier hopped up, and pressing his back against the curve of her stomach, listened intently as Alison began to read aloud.

Santo and his wife invited Dizzy, Gina, and Alison to their trailer for a barbecue dinner. Alison immediately felt at home with Renzo and his younger brothers. She helped them fix their hamburgers, and later, despite the heat, she took them all outside to play soccer. It beat sitting around the trailer, watching the grown-ups talk and drink coffee.

Later, back at Dizzy's, Alison and Gina looked through old photo albums for a while. "That was Dizzy's husband," Gina said, pointing to a sad-faced clown on bended knee before her aunt, a beautiful ballerina. "They were the best. Star turns, right, Diz?"

Dizzy nudged her niece good-naturedly. "Hey, you could be nice and say now I'*m* the best"

"Why would I say *that*?" Gina smiled wryly and batted her eyelashes. "You're the best, not me. All these summers here and I still haven't even performed yet."

"Your choice not mine, Babycakes."

"You're kidding," Alison said. "You're amazing up there, Gina. Totally awesome."

"Yes, she is," Dizzy said. "Which reminds me." She searched for something in a drawer near the television. When she returned, she pulled a heart-shaped locket from a little velvet bag. "For you," she said, handing it to Gina. "For your first performance. To give you heart. It's an old family tradition." She helped Gina open the clasp. "Those are your great-great-grandparents."

"Isn't it more like a superstition?" Gina asked. "That's what my mom says, and then she makes this face. You know the one." Gina rolled her eyes, apparently imitating her mother.

"Yes, I guess I do. Well, call it what you like." Dizzy shrugged. "As long as you wear it, what's the difference?"

Gina nodded, then gave her aunt a quick hug.

"Off to bed with you now. There's a clean nightie and towels in the second drawer," Dizzy told Alison. "I'll sleep out here."

"Thanks."

"Alison?" Dizzy caught her hand as she turned to go. "Do you mind me calling you Speedo, hon?"

"Not a bit." Alison smiled mysteriously. "But you haven't seen anything yet, Diz. Just wait till tomorrow. Monty and me, we're going to be the speediest learners in Circus Corbellini history. And just in the nick of time."

Chapter
Seven

MONTY SAVES THE DAY

F rom the moment Alison entered the big top to practice the next day, she sensed that something was different. The air, while still humid, crackled with a force that seemed almost electric. Was she the only one who felt it? Magda's moldy hay smell still lingered in the tent, tickling Alison's nose. She hoped she wouldn't sneeze while she was trying to balance. Monty sat below the low wire, alert and expectant.

Alison took a hesitant step forward. The wire seemed

alive with a strange and beautiful energy. Was this the "song of the cable" that The Great Moreno had written of? "Let me try it without the pole," she said to Dizzy.

"I don't think you're ready but . . ." Dizzy broke off with a shrug.

Alison took another step and another. A voice inside her head—The Great Moreno's?—kept urging her on. She felt as surefooted as if she were walking across a basketball court! Her eyes didn't leave her goal for an instant, yet somehow, from their sharp intakes of breath, she could picture Dizzy's and Gina's astonishment.

"Incredible," Dizzy whispered. "This is unheard of. Gina, run! Go get Poppa. He has to see this."

In the middle of the wire, The Great Moreno's voice told Alison to stop and kneel, and she obeyed without thinking. As she lowered her right knee onto the cable and gave The Great Moreno's distinctive salute, a man's voice boomed from the nearest tent flap.

"San Giuseppe!" Poppa Corbellini exclaimed. "She is the image of The Great Moreno!"

Alison grinned as she continued her crossing. Just one more trick ought to do it, she thought. Near the other end, she called to Ellie's terrier. "Monty, up!" As the dog climbed the stepladder, Alison inched toward the platform. Then, as she stepped onto it and made two

kissing sounds, he leaped into her arms.

"See, Dizzy?" said Alison as she jumped down with Monty. "Didn't I tell you we were fast learners?"

"Yes, but this! Even a child born and raised in the circus couldn't do it!" Dizzy's dark eye makeup seemed to underline her amazement. "Poppa, she must do this in the show."

"About the show," Alison began, and Gina urged Poppa Corbellini closer. "I think I know a way to convince those guys to give you the money."

From the way the head of the circus family raised his eyebrows at Dizzy and Gina, Alison knew that the three Corbellinis were suddenly all ears.

All that day Dizzy worried aloud about the weather, though Alison couldn't really tell whether she was hoping for rain or not. At dinner Dizzy complained about not having practiced much, and in the middle of the night Alison heard her cry out. But Dizzy waved away Alison's concern and said she'd only stubbed her toe.

The next morning, after eating breakfast and stretching, Dizzy

disappeared into the bedroom. In the main part of the
trailer, Gina helped Alison into her costume, fixed
her hair, and fastened the crown. "Alison," she said, "*you
should wear the locket.*"

"No way. Dizzy gave it to you." Alison wondered
whether Gina was disappointed that Alison was
performing in her place. If she is, she thought, she's
doing a great job of hiding it.

"Please? Wear it for luck or whatever. Not that I'm
superstitious or anything. But just in case."

"All right," said Alison. "If you insist."

When Dizzy finally waddled out of the back room
in oversize shoes, she was dressed more like a sad-faced
clown than a wire walker. Alison gaped, not knowing
quite what to say. She was reminded of the old photos
Dizzy had shown her. Then she looked more closely
at Dizzy's wardrobe. "That's just like your husband's,
isn't it?" she asked.

Dizzy's lips formed a smile within the painted-on
frown. "Very observant, Speedo. It is his, actually. My way
of keeping him in the act." She turned to Gina. "You'd
better hurry up and get dressed, Babycakes. A performer
is always prepared."

"Aunt Diz," Gina protested, rolling her eyes, "you know
I'm not going on."

"No arguments. You just never know." Dizzy looked at Alison.

Suddenly, a whole swarm of butterflies went crazy in Alison's stomach. "Listen to Dizzy, Gina," Alison began. "You just never—" The sentence hung there, unfinished, as Alison dashed madly to the bathroom with not a moment to spare.

Before long, the festive smells of popcorn, roasted peanuts, and cotton candy— floss, Dizzy called it—spilled out of the big top and into the backyard. Taped circus music blared from the speakers. Magda and her trainer made their way slowly toward the tent, both dressed in sequins and satin and huge fake jewels. As show time neared, Alison could almost feel the crowd's pulse throb along with her own.

As Alison and Dizzy waited for their music cue, taking care to avoid the guy wires, Gina paced back and forth nearby. Every once in a while, she'd stop, pet Monty, and ask Alison, "Are you sure you're okay?"

Alison nodded weakly, not wanting to admit her own doubt. What if The Great Moreno wasn't with her today?

True, Poppa Corbellini had agreed to let her perform only on the low wire. If she lost her balance, she didn't have far to fall, but still—the last thing she wanted to do was mess up—Circus Corbellini was depending on her.

Peeking through the tent flaps, Alison gazed longingly up at the high wire where Dizzy was to perform. By comparison, her low wire looked pretty disappointing. If only they were using a net today, maybe she could have performed up there, too. But all of Dizzy's props made relying on trained spotters a safer option. That was hard for Alison to believe, until Poppa Corbellini had explained: landing in a net on a prop—an umbrella or a balance pole—was actually more dangerous than landing on a spotter who broke a fall by flinging themselves into special positions. Still, even without a net, Alison thought, that high wire was calling her. "Oh, Dizzy, please can't I—" She broke off as an unmistakable grimace of pain crossed Dizzy's face. "What's wrong?"

"It's nothing." Again Dizzy winced.

Gina frowned at her aunt. "Is it your arthritis? Is that what's hurting you?"

Dizzy nodded. "That and my pride, Babycakes."

"No way you're going on, then," Gina said. "There's too much at stake to risk a fall, especially in front of *this* audience."

Dizzy sighed. "I guess you're right. I can lie to myself, but not to the wire."

"Gina can go on for you!" Alison said. "She's great up there."

Gina opened her mouth to say something, but Dizzy wrapped her niece in a bear hug, and the matter was settled. Monty yipped softly.

"Shhhh!" Alison told him. "You don't want to scare Magda, do you, boy?"

Monty whimpered in reply, then perked up his ears at the sound of the music being played. Suddenly Alison realized that it was the wire walkers' cue!

"Gina, we're on," she whispered, holding tight to Monty. "I guess you're first, huh? Good luck!"

"Thanks." Gina smiled weakly, squeezed Dizzy's hand, and ducked into the big top.

Alison parted the flaps, and with Dizzy beside her, watched the high wire expectantly. Licking her lips, she fidgeted with her costume. When she felt the locket beneath her leotard, she turned to Dizzy, her eyes wide. "Diz, the locket! Gina's not wearing it!" she whispered.

"Good thing she doesn't believe in that stuff," Dizzy said. "It's too late now."

Alison's heart beat fast as she watched Gina climb the rigging.

Chapter Eight

DRAWING THE SPOTLIGHT

Poppa Corbellini, poised below the high wire as Gina's spotter, seemed surprised to see her. Alison knew he'd been expecting Dizzy the Clown. Could one old man really catch her if she fell? "I still think a net would be safer," Alison whispered.

"Not at this height, hon. Spotters know what they're doing." When Alison's mouth twitched to one side, Dizzy added, "You've got to remember, that's family they're protecting."

The spotlight followed Gina up to the platform.
One of her teenage cousins played a long drum roll. Gina
struck a pose and smiled down at the crowd, and the
taped music for Dizzy's act began. But Gina didn't move.

Dizzy tugged at Alison's arm and hurried closer to
the rigging. She motioned to Gina to continue. The girl
nodded and stepped forward, but her foot never met
the wire. Instead, she stood there frozen, from her smile
right down to her pointed toes.

"Oh, no!" Alison gasped. Somewhere behind her,
a man muttered softly in Italian. It's the locket, Alison
thought. It had to be, because in practice Gina was
perfect. But now, with the crowd and the spotlight . . .

"Monty," Alison whispered, "we've got to do
something!" Turning, she saw Dizzy's brother "Santo,
spot me," she hissed. "Diz, get the light off her, okay?
And make that announcement, just like we planned."

"No, Alison, you can't possibly . . . "

But Alison pretended not to hear Dizzy's protest.
She raced to oak ladder, commanding Monty to sit
at the bottom. Still wearing her cape, she began to
climb. "Oh, please," she whispered to herself, "let me
still be able to do this."

Suddenly, the spotlight was on her. As Alison reached
the platform across from Gina, Dizzy cleared her throat at

the microphone. Everything stopped—the taped music, the crunch of peanut shells and popcorn, and for a moment, Alison feared, her own heartbeat as well.

"Ladies and gentlemen, honored guests." Dizzy paused. "As you know, Circus Corbellini plans to embark on an exciting new adventure—bringing the circus into your schools. We believe that all children can be successful, from kindergarten right up through high school. Let us help them discover that ability to succeed.

"And now, I take great pride in presenting a young student who came here just days ago, wanting to walk the wire. Her progress has been extraordinary, to say the least. Just look at how proudly she holds herself. That, more than circus skills themselves, is what we're after. Ladies and gentlemen, Miss Alison Speedo McCann!"

Alison took a deep breath, removed her cape, and checked for Santo in position below. Then she concentrated on Gina's feet, her target at the end of the wire. Gina herself looked more concerned for Alison than scared for herself. Okay, here goes, Alison thought. She only hoped The Great Moreno would still be with her.

But as her foot found the cable, her arms flailed frantically. The whole crowd drew a breath. Alison swallowed hard. Focus, she told herself. Concentrate. Stay in the moment. She willed her other foot forward. Find the balance. She took another step, and another. Her eyes never wavered from Gina's feet. As curious as she was to see the crowd's reaction, she knew that looking down could mean disaster. By the time she reached the halfway point of her crossing, she had found the "song of the wire." Surely she could make it easily to the other side. But Gina was still on the platform, and Alison didn't want to embarrass her by forcing her back into the spotlight.

Turn around, The Great Moreno seemed to whisper. *Go back.*

But I've never done this, Alison wanted to shout.

Trust yourself. Rise on the balls of your feet. Let your heels swivel and meet the wire again.

Alison obeyed. As she neared her platform again, she called down to the terrier. "Monty, come!" Eagerly, he started up the ladder. As she took her final step onto the platform, he reached the top. "And up!" Alison blew him two kisses, and he leaped into her arms. The applause felt better than any she'd ever received for sinking a basket from center court.

That glow followed her even as she tucked Monty close and started down. She'd never realized before how hard it was to descend a ladder using one arm.

At the bottom, Dizzy rushed to meet her. She seemed to be beaming. "The business people gave me a thumbs-up!" she whispered hoarsely. "You did it!"

"No, we did it. Hey, Diz, look!" Alison pointed up at the high wire, now back in the spotlight. "Can you believe it? Gina's doing her whole routine!"

When Gina finished, Alison and Dizzy clapped and cheered right along with the rest of the audience.

Later, back at Dizzy's trailer, Alison took the locket off and handed it to Gina. "So what happened up there, anyway?" she asked gently. "You should have been wearing the locket. And I should have—"

Gina only shrugged, but Dizzy cut in. "Performance anxiety, I'll bet that's what it was," she said, shaking her head. "All these summers—I should have understood, Gina. You were that way when you were a little girl. Remember that piano recital? The gymnastics meet?"

Gina blushed and hung her head.

"Hey, it's nothing to be ashamed of," Alison said. "I know a girl like that at school. Her body tells her she's afraid at meets, and then, bingo, she is! It's like her mind believes her. She's better now, though. Some kind of doctor helped her. A specialist."

Gina nodded and managed a weak smile. "Yeah, I guess everybody needs help with something."

"Hey, you know what?" Alison said. "I think I'm kind of like that with reading. For me, though, it sure is hard to admit I have a problem."

"Me, too," Dizzy said.

"Me, three," added Gina, and Alison laughed. Someone, maybe Keisha, had said those same words after the Magic Attic Club's first adventure.

With a wistful sigh, Alison picked up Monty, knowing it was time to go. Then she hugged Dizzy and Gina. "I mean it, this has been great. You've been like family to me," she said. "But speaking of family, I think I'd better go back to mine—and to school." She snapped her fingers. "Hey, you never know, maybe sometime Circus Corbellini will come to Lincoln Elementary! With Magda, I hope."

Dizzy and Gina stood waving good-bye for the longest time. But finally, Alison headed off through the rows of trailers toward the circus wagon, and the mirror that would take her back to Ellie Goodwin's attic.

Chapter

Nine

THE WORDS

One moment Alison was waiting to be alone in front of the circus wagon's mirror. The next, she and Monty were standing before Ellie's tall, gilded one in the familiar attic. Outside, darkness was gathering, and she knew she'd better hurry home. After changing quickly into her clothes, she grabbed the key and clattered downstairs.

Monty tore through the house, yipping for Ellie. Apparently, she hadn't returned yet. Alison scratched behind the terrier's ears. "Thanks for coming with me, boy. That was fun, wasn't it? I'll have to tell Ellie all about it when I see her."

Monty only sneezed. But after Alison locked the front door and hid the house key, she glimpsed his little black nose pressed tight against the front window as if to say good-bye.

Alison couldn't believe how tired she was. With school starting the next day, at least she had a good excuse to go to bed early. Otherwise her mother would have wondered if she were sick. Alison tried to relive each moment with the circus, but sleep came too quickly. The last thing she recalled thinking about was her final talk with Dizzy and Gina, and how she, Alison Speedo McCann, had still not said The Words.

"Alison, you're late," said Heather the next morning when they met on the sidewalk in front of the McCanns'. "Don't tell me you overslept. Not on the first day of school."

Alison shook her head. "Sorry. I looked at the clock wrong."

"Keisha went on to Megan's. We'll meet them there, okay?"

Alison nodded and slung her

nearly empty backpack over one shoulder. Mrs. Haggerty would probably have plenty of books to put in there after school. "Sorry I didn't get done in time to meet you guys up in the attic," she said at last. "I went later, though. And took Monty through the mirror."

"Omigosh!" Heather's dark eyes grew wide. "You're kidding! Wish we'd thought of that. So, tell. What did you do? Where'd you go?"

"To the circus," Alison said. "And it's a good thing you didn't take Monty. I needed him for part of my act." And then, even though she knew she'd soon repeat the whole story to Megan and Keisha, Alison told Heather every last detail. Or so she thought. It wasn't until they reached Megan's that Alison realized she'd left one important thing out.

"Hey, Ali!" Keisha grinned. "We thought you'd never get here."

"Couldn't decide what skirt to wear, huh?" teased Megan and everyone laughed, even Alison. She bet none of them could even remember the last time she'd worn a skirt to school. "Seriously," Megan continued, "we've been dying to tell you what we decided to wear when we went to the attic."

"Okay, okay," Alison said. "But let me say something first, before I chicken out."

Her friends waited for Alison to go on.

"Over the summer I had to go see this specialist, and . . . well, I don't know why exactly, but I just couldn't make myself tell you guys. At least, not until now." Alison sighed. "I mean, nobody's perfect, right? Sooner or later, everybody needs help with something."

Heather, Megan, and Keisha gathered around, their faces suddenly tight with concern. "What specialist, Ali? Are you sick?" asked Keisha.

"You're scaring us," Megan added.

"Is there anything we can do?" Heather asked.

"No, no. You don't understand." Alison realized at once that she'd misled them without meaning to. And all because she was too proud to say two stupid little words. "I'm not dying or anything."

"But you said . . ." Keisha frowned.

"I saw a specialist, all right," replied Alison. "A reading specialist. Turns out I don't just have a problem with reading. I've got a reading disability." There. She'd said it. She searched her friends' faces for a hint of pity. All she saw was relief, and then . . .

"Oh, Ali, that's great!" Heather exclaimed. "Now you can get help, right?"

"Do you have a tutor?" asked Keisha.

Alison answered them both with a quick nod. I can't

believe I made such a big thing of this, she thought.

"No wonder reading's been so hard for you," said Megan. "I know just how frustrating that is."

Alison opened her mouth in astonishment. Megan? The best reader in their entire grade? "You're kidding, right? There's no way you could . . . " Alison's voice trailed off as Megan turned her back for a moment.

"Ta-da!" When Megan spun around, arms raised like Gina's on the platform, her green eyes sparkled behind a pair of gold-framed glasses. "Aren't they great?"

she said. "I've been dying to surprise you."

"Megan, you look so cool in them!" Heather seemed almost envious.

"When did you get those?" asked Alison. "How did you know you needed them?"

"Like I said, reading's been hard for me lately."

Alison nodded, and, for the first time in weeks, fell fully in step with her three best friends.

Diary

Dear ~~Dairy~~ Diary,

See? Two sessions with Mrs. Haggerty and I'm already making progress! At her house, she lets me use this computer program that helps a lot. I told Heather, Megan, and Alison about it, and we checked to see if the Media Center at school has it, too. It doesn't. And wouldn't you know, the program's really expensive and there's not enough money in the budget to buy a copy this year.

But if you think that's <u>bad</u> news, you're wrong. Leave it to the Magic Attic Club to come up with a great idea. After I told Keisha and Megan about my wire-walking adventure with the circus, I could almost see their ~~brians~~ — make that brains—start spinning. You never know what kind of help your friends can give you once you tell them you've got a problem.

Anyway, here's the plan. First, we invite a circus to Lincoln Elementary and have them teach us tricks in gym class. Then, at the end of the term, we put on this big show. I bet that'd raise lots of money for the Media Center. And wouldn't it be cool to show off for everybody we know?

All four of us had to go to the Parent-Teacher Group meeting and tell them our idea. We divided it up fair and square so we all had equal parts. But I could tell even Keisha was scared to go up there in front of all those people.

When it was my turn, I got a funny feeling in my stomach, and for a minute I thought about making a run for it. But I talked to myself like The Great Moreno did when I was up on that high wire: Focus. Concentrate. Step-by-step.

And so, sentence-by-sentence, I read my

part of the speech in front of everybody. At the end I threw in a little extra thing we hadn't talked about. I said, "Imagine how you'd feel to see your kid on the high wire." Then I walked one of the floor planks like it was a cable. At the pretend platform, I made a victory salute. Everybody cheered, especially Heather, Megan, and Keisha.

Right after that, the grown-ups voted on how to spend the magazine sale money and guess what? The circus got a big grant! I have no idea where to find Circus Corbellini, but you can bet the Magic Attic Club will be in the library, trying to find out.

Love, Me!

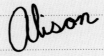